WHISPERS OVER W

A Family's Feud

Gary Ogden

Table Of Contents

Chapter 1

The Heart of Windermere

Eleanor Ellis sat in a dimly lit room, staring out at Lake Windermere. The water's shimmer seemed to dance with memories, each ripple a reminder of years gone by. The scent of fresh scones wafted from the kitchen, filling "Windermere Wonders" with a homely aroma that had greeted guests for decades.

She held a letter in her trembling hand, its content weighing on her more than she cared to admit. Dr. Patrick's words were gentle but firm, a prognosis she had feared. Terminal illness. Time was running out.

"Mother?" Julia's voice, filled with concern, broke Eleanor's thoughts. She entered the room, her apron stained with the day's culinary endeavors. Behind her trailed Martin, always in his crisp suits, and Daniel, with a worry line that seemed to deepen each day.

"What is it?" Martin asked, his voice tinged with impatience. He always was the restless one. Eleanor cleared her throat, folding the letter. "It's nothing," she replied, her voice betraying her attempt at nonchalance.

Julia approached, taking a seat next to her mother. "You've been distant lately. What's bothering you?"

Eleanor looked into Julia's eyes, so full of passion and fire, so much like her own at that age. "It's the future of this place," she began, her gaze drifting to the restaurant's entrance, where a young Sophie was giggling, taking orders from regulars. "I've been thinking of what happens after... after I'm gone."

Martin frowned, shifting uncomfortably. "Mother, we've been through this. I've been handling the finances for years. It only makes sense—"

Julia interrupted, her tone sharp. "This place is as much mine as it is yours. I pour my soul into every dish. You can't just claim it."

Eleanor sighed, feeling the weight of the rift between her children. "This isn't about who did what," she whispered. "It's about preserving our legacy."

Daniel, ever the peacemaker, intervened, "We'll figure it out, Eleanor. We always do."

As the four shared a moment of fragile unity, an unfamiliar face peered through the window, observing, evaluating. It was Graham Lynch, and he had plans of his own.

Chapter 2

Tensions at the Table

The evening was in full swing at "Windermere Wonders." Guests were lost in the world of flavors Julia masterfully crafted. Eleanor, despite her ailment, still loved to mingle with the guests, some of whom had become friends over the years.

Sophie, balancing a tray of appetizers, gracefully moved between tables, her youth and energy a stark contrast to the dark wood and historical portraits that adorned the walls. "Table seven sends their compliments to the chef, Aunt Julia!" she called out, winking.

Julia smiled but was quickly drawn into a whispered conversation with Daniel. "We need to talk about the offers," Daniel muttered, discreetly nodding towards a corner where Martin sat, deep in conversation with the very same Graham Lynch.

Julia frowned, "Already making deals? We promised Mother we'd hold off until she..." Her voice trailed off, the unspoken words heavy in the air.

Across the room, Martin's face was a mask of politeness, but his eyes betrayed his interest. "Mr. Lynch, while I appreciate your generous offer, now isn't the time."

Graham leaned back, his smile not quite reaching his eyes. "Martin, the offer stands for now, but opportunities like these are fleeting. Your family restaurant has charm, history, and I see potential."

"Potential to be turned into one of your modern, soulless chains?" Martin retorted, his restraint waning.

Graham laughed softly, raising an eyebrow, "There's a lot of money in 'soulless' these days."

Eleanor, having overheard fragments of their conversation, approached the duo, her face stern. "Mr. Lynch," she began, her voice firm despite her frailty, "Windermere Wonders isn't just a business. It's our home, our heart. And it's not for sale."

As Graham made his exit, offering a polite nod, Eleanor turned to Martin, "Promise me you won't let him destroy what we've built."

Martin sighed, avoiding her gaze, "I promise, Mother."

The evening drew to a close, but as the lights dimmed and the guests departed, the challenges facing the Ellis family were only just beginning.

Chapter 3

A Mysterious Offer

The morning after the eventful evening was shrouded in mist, casting a hazy blanket over the Lake District. Inside "Windermere Wonders," Martin sat alone, nursing his coffee, the previous night's conversation with Graham Lynch playing on his mind.

The restaurant was quiet in the mornings, a silent testament to the bustling activity it would soon host. As Martin gazed out, he noticed a familiar figure approaching. It was Graham, looking even more out of place in the daylight with his city attire contrasting starkly against the rustic charm of Windermere.

Martin tensed but motioned for him to come in. "Back again, Mr. Lynch?" he remarked dryly. "I thought my mother made our position quite clear."

Graham chuckled, taking a seat opposite Martin. "Your mother is a formidable woman," he began, "but business is business. And I believe every man has his price."

Martin's eyes narrowed. "And what makes you so sure I can be bought?"

Graham leaned forward, placing an envelope on the table. "This is an initial offer, Martin. Just a starting point for negotiations."

Martin hesitated for a moment before opening the envelope. His eyes widened at the figure. It was generous, even by his standards. The amount was enough to ensure a comfortable life for the family, without the stress of managing the restaurant.

Graham watched his reaction closely. "Think about it. This is your ticket out. A chance to explore opportunities beyond these walls."

Martin looked conflicted. "This restaurant has been in our family for generations. It's not just bricks and mortar, it's memories, it's legacy."

Graham nodded understandingly, "I respect that. But consider this - holding onto something doesn't always mean progress. Sometimes it's the weight that holds you back."

Just then, Julia walked in, her face hardening upon seeing Graham. "What's he doing here, Martin?" she demanded, her tone icy.

Martin sighed, "Discussing business."

Graham rose, tipping his hat slightly to Julia. "Always a pleasure, Ms. Ellis. Martin, take your time to consider. Opportunities like this don't knock often." With that, he exited, leaving a palpable tension in his wake.

Julia glared at the envelope, then at her brother. "You're not seriously considering this, are you?"

Martin sighed deeply, rubbing his temples. "I don't know, Jules. I just... don't know."

Chapter 4

The Heartbeat of the Kitchen

Julia had always considered the kitchen the soul of "Windermere Wonders." It was where she felt most alive, orchestrating a symphony of flavors, creating dishes that told stories. But that morning, as she stepped in, something felt amiss.

She could sense it—a strange tension, an unease in the air, like a discordant note in her otherwise harmonious domain. Daniel was already there, prepping ingredients, his brow furrowed in concentration. Sophie, her niece, was humming a tune, but even her usually infectious energy seemed subdued.

"What's happened?" Julia questioned, her gaze scanning the room.

Sophie hesitated, then pointed at the stove. "Look."

Julia approached and instantly noticed. Her grandmother's old, beloved saucepan—a family heirloom—was ruined. Its bottom was charred, and a burnt smell wafted through the air.

"That was no accident," Daniel murmured, looking up from his work. "That saucepan has been here longer than any of us. Someone did this deliberately."

Julia's heart raced. She tried to calm herself, refusing to jump to conclusions. "Perhaps it was just negligence. These things happen."

Sophie shook her head, her young face marred with worry. "Aunt Jules, it's not just the saucepan. Look at the orders." She handed Julia a notepad, where the evening's reservations were scribbled. Several bookings had been crossed out. "They called to cancel. All of them mentioned getting a better offer from a new place in town."

Julia's mind raced, piecing the puzzle together. "Lynch," she whispered.

Daniel sighed. "We don't know that for sure. But someone is trying to sabotage us."

She took a deep breath, summoning her strength. "We'll get through this. We always do." Her determined gaze met Sophie's. "Prepare the special for tonight. And you," she said, turning to Daniel, "help me recreate grandmother's sauce with that new set of pans we got last month."

Throughout the day, the kitchen was a hive of activity. Julia, with her indomitable spirit, led the charge, creating masterpieces from scratch. The staff, inspired by her resilience, rallied around, their loyalty unwavering.

By evening, "Windermere Wonders" was ready to welcome its guests, the setback transformed into a challenge overcome. Yet, in the shadows, the question lingered: Who wanted the Ellis legacy to crumble, and why?

Chapter 5

Whispers in the Wind

As night fell over Windermere, the calmness of the lake was juxtaposed by the tense atmosphere inside the restaurant. Despite the challenges faced earlier, the place was relatively full, and guests were enjoying their meals, mostly unaware of the behind-the-scenes drama.

Eleanor, using the staircase's handrail as support, made her way down from her room above the restaurant. She felt a responsibility to be present, to showcase the unity of the Ellis family during trying times.

In the dining area, she found Martin, standing by the entrance and greeting guests with his usual charm. She approached him, concern evident in her eyes. "Martin," she began, her voice soft, "I've been hearing whispers. About Lynch, about offers, and about selling."

He looked away, discomfort evident. "Mother, this isn't the time or place."

She gently touched his arm. "It's always the time when family is involved. Tell me the truth."

Martin sighed, leading her to a quiet corner. "Lynch made an offer. A substantial one," he admitted. "But before you say anything, I haven't made a decision."

Eleanor stared at him, her expression inscrutable. "Do you remember the tales your grandfather used to tell? About how this place was his dream, his passion?"

Martin nodded. "Of course. But times change, Mother. Dreams also evolve. Maybe this is our chance to dream bigger."

She smiled sadly, "Sometimes, dreams found in our roots are far more precious than those in uncharted skies."

Their conversation was interrupted by Sophie, who hurried over, her face pale. "Aunt Julia needs you both in the kitchen. Now."

They found Julia at the kitchen's entrance, a note clutched in her hand. Her face was a mix of anger and concern. "This was left on the backdoor," she said, handing the note to Eleanor.

The note, written in an unfamiliar, jagged handwriting, read: "Stop while you're ahead. Windermere won't be wonderful for long."

Eleanor's grip tightened on the note. "We're being threatened."

Martin frowned, "It might be just a prank."

Julia scoffed, "Burnt pans, canceled reservations, and now this? It's too calculated for a prank."

Eleanor took a deep breath, "We need help. It's time to involve the authorities."

They all nodded in agreement. Little did they know, their decision to seek help would lead them to Detective Ian McAllister, a man with a keen sense for mysteries, especially ones intertwined with personal vendettas.

Chapter 6

A Detective in Windermere

The next morning, the tranquil scenery of the Lake District was in stark contrast to the unease that had settled in the heart of "Windermere Wonders." As Eleanor had decided, the authorities were contacted, and Detective Ian McAllister was assigned to the case. His reputation preceded him; tales of his uncanny ability to solve complex mysteries were well-known throughout the county.

Ian, a tall man with graying hair and sharp, observant eyes, entered the restaurant, the morning sun casting long shadows on the wooden floor. Eleanor, accompanied by Julia and Martin, greeted him.

"Detective McAllister," Eleanor began, offering a firm handshake, "thank you for coming on such short notice."

Ian nodded, "From what I've heard, time is of the essence. Let's get down to the details."

Julia handed him the threatening note, her hands slightly trembling. "This is just the tip of the iceberg. There have been incidents, attempts to sabotage our business."

Ian examined the note carefully. "This handwriting... it's intentionally shaky, meant to throw off any identification."

Martin chimed in, "We have our suspicions about who might be behind this. A man named Graham Lynch."

Ian raised an eyebrow, "The real estate mogul?"

"Yes," Eleanor replied, her tone bitter. "He's been quite persistent in buying us out."

Ian made a note. "Any direct confrontations or threats from him?"

Julia hesitated, "Not threats, per se, but he has a way of making his ambitions quite clear."

The detective paced thoughtfully for a moment. "I'll look into Mr. Lynch's activities, but it's important to remember that jumping to conclusions can be perilous."

As they conversed, Sophie approached with a tray of fresh pastries and tea. "Thought you might need some refreshments," she offered with a hesitant smile.

"Thank you, Miss..." Ian began.

"Sophie," she replied. "Just Sophie."

Ian smiled, a warmth in his eyes that contrasted with his otherwise stoic demeanor. "Thank you, Sophie."

After discussing further details and ensuring the family's safety, Ian decided to inspect the restaurant's surroundings. Eleanor watched him as he methodically surveyed the area, her mind grappling with the uncertainty of their situation.

Julia turned to her mother, "Do you trust him?"

Eleanor considered the question. "I believe he's our best shot at getting to the bottom of this."

And as Ian disappeared into the misty shores of Windermere, the game of cat and mouse had officially begun.

Chapter 7

Shadows of the Past

Detective Ian McAllister found himself standing at the edge of the lake, the tranquil waters reflecting the pastel hues of the setting sun. The scenic beauty was captivating, but he was more intrigued by the murmurs of the village, the undertones of stories intertwined with "Windermere Wonders."

He decided to visit the local pub, "The Shepherd's Crook," a cozy place frequented by locals. The wooden walls, adorned with photographs from bygone eras, whispered tales from the past.

As Ian entered, he drew a few curious glances. His reputation meant his face was known to many. John, the pub's owner, greeted him warmly. "Detective McAllister! Didn't expect to see you here. What brings you to Windermere?"

Ian took a seat at the bar, accepting the glass of ale offered. "A case, John. I believe you might be able to help."

John leaned forward, intrigued. "Oh? What's it about?"

Ian began, "It's about the Ellis family and the recent troubles at their restaurant. I've heard whispers that there might be more to the story than what's visible on the surface."

John sighed, his jovial expression dimming. "Ah, the Ellis family. They've been pillars of this community for generations. Their restaurant is more than just a business; it's a legacy. But every legacy has its shadows."

Ian perked up. "Shadows?"

John hesitated, then began, "Years ago, before Eleanor took over, there was a feud between the Ellis family and the Lynches. Old Mr. Lynch and Eleanor's father were close friends, but a bad business deal tore them apart. It became so bitter that they stopped speaking to each other. The younger Lynch, Graham, grew up hearing about it."

Ian's mind raced, connecting the dots. "So, Graham's interest in the restaurant..."

"Could be more than just business," John finished Ian's sentence. "It could be an old vendetta, rekindled."

Just then, an old man from a corner table, who had been eavesdropping, chimed in. "Don't forget the night of the fire!"

John's face turned a shade paler. "Right. Years ago, there was a mysterious fire at the restaurant. It was rebuilt, but the culprit was never found. Rumors said it was tied to the feud, but nothing was ever proven."

Ian took a moment to digest the information. "This adds a whole new dimension to the case. Thank you, John. And to you as well," he nodded at the old man.

As Ian stepped out into the night, the weight of the past loomed heavily. The case wasn't just about threats and a potential buyout. It was about old wounds, rivalries, and the shadows that lurk behind family legacies.

*C*hapter 8

Unearthing Old Secrets

The next morning, the sun glistened over Windermere's waters, but the village was awash with anticipation. Rumors of Detective McAllister's visit to "The Shepherd's Crook" had spread, rekindling memories of the old feud and the fire that had nearly razed "Windermere Wonders" to the ground.

Inside the restaurant, Eleanor sat in her private study, a room filled with old photographs, letters, and mementos. There was a knock on the door, and Julia entered, holding a worn-out leather-bound diary.

"Mother," she began, her voice trembling slightly, "I think it's time we revisit grandfather's diary. If the past is catching up with us, we need to be prepared."

Eleanor nodded, taking a deep breath. "I haven't opened that diary since he passed away. But you're right; we need to face our history."

Together, they began to sift through the pages, filled with the elegant cursive of Eleanor's father. The diary was a testament to his dreams, aspirations, and the challenges he faced. Midway through, they stumbled upon an entry dated a week before the mysterious fire.

"Met with L. today. He's insistent on the merger. I don't trust him anymore, not after the betrayal. There's something he's not telling me."

Julia looked at Eleanor, her eyes wide. "L. must be Lynch's father."

Eleanor read on, her voice shaking, "'there's talk of a secret, something that could change the fate of Windermere Wonders. L. warned me about a storm coming. I have to protect this legacy, for Eleanor and Julia.'"

A chill ran down Julia's spine. "Mother, do you think he knew about the fire?"

Eleanor shook her head, tears forming in her eyes. "I don't know. All these years, we've tried to move forward, to leave the past behind. But it seems the past isn't done with us."

Suddenly, there was another knock. Martin, looking agitated, stood at the doorway. "Detective McAllister is here. He wants to speak with both of you."

In the dining area, Detective McAllister sat with a cup of tea, his sharp gaze scanning the room. "Mrs. Ellis, Miss Julia," he nodded as they approached. "I've been doing some digging, and it seems the roots of this case go deeper than we imagined."

Julia held out the diary. "You might want to read this, Detective."

As Ian delved into the diary's contents, the atmosphere grew tense. Each revelation made it clear that the current threats to "Windermere Wonders" were tied to a web of secrets, betrayal, and old rivalries.

Ian finally looked up, determination evident in his eyes. "We're not just solving a mystery here; we're unearthing the soul of this village. And I promise you, we will get to the bottom of this."

$\mathcal{C}$hapter 9

The Ghosts of Grasmere

Windermere was not the only village in the Lake District with tales to tell. Not far away, nestled among the rolling hills and lush meadows, was Grasmere, another village steeped in history. It was to this village that Detective McAllister headed next, having learned of a possible link between the Ellis family's troubles and an old property dispute in Grasmere.

Upon arriving, Ian was greeted by the scent of blooming flowers and the distant hum of village life. He headed straight to Grasmere's historical society, housed in a quaint, ivy-covered building. There, he met Agatha, the society's elderly curator, a woman who had lived in Grasmere her entire life and knew its stories like the back of her hand.

"Detective McAllister," Agatha greeted, adjusting her spectacles. "I've heard about your work in Windermere. What brings you to our peaceful village?"

"I'm investigating a series of events tied to the Ellis family," Ian began, producing the diary. "This diary mentions a secret related to Grasmere. I believe it's tied to a property dispute from years ago."

Agatha's expression changed, a hint of sadness clouding her eyes. "Ah, the old Greenwood estate. It's a tragic tale. The property once belonged to the Greenwoods, a close ally of the Ellis family. But after a series of unfortunate events, the estate ended up in the hands of the Lynches."

Ian leaned forward, intrigued. "What events?"

Agatha took a deep breath, her voice turning somber. "There was an accident, or so it was termed. The youngest Greenwood, Lily, was found drowned in the lake on their property. The estate was heavily mortgaged, and with no heir, it eventually fell into the hands of the bank. The Lynches, always having an eye on that land, acquired it soon after."

"Was the death ever investigated?"

Agatha nodded slowly. "It was, but it was ruled an accident. However, many in Grasmere believe there was foul play involved. The Greenwood estate was prime land, and the Lynches, especially the older Lynch, would have done anything to get their hands on it."

Ian processed the information, the pieces of the puzzle slowly coming together. "Could the secret mentioned in the diary be related to Lily Greenwood's death?"

Agatha hesitated before replying. "It's possible. The Ellis family and the Greenwoods were very close. If there was any suspicion of foul play, they would have known."

Ian stood up, determination in his eyes. "I need to visit the Greenwood estate. Can you guide me there?"

Agatha nodded, a mixture of hope and trepidation on her face. "Of course, Detective. But be careful. The ghosts of

Grasmere have a way of resurfacing when you least expect them."

As Ian set out to explore the Greenwood estate, he knew he was delving into a chapter of history that many wanted to remain closed. But the truth, no matter how old or buried, had a way of shining through.

Chapter 10

Echoes of Greenwood Estate

The Greenwood estate, though abandoned for years, still held an air of grandeur. Towering oaks, ancient witnesses to countless secrets, lined the path leading to the mansion. The once magnificent home now looked forlorn, its windows shuttered and ivy creeping up its stone walls.

As Detective McAllister and Agatha approached, the creaking of the old Iron Gate echoed eerily in the stillness. "It's been years since I've been here," Agatha murmured, her eyes scanning the surroundings with a mixture of nostalgia and apprehension.

Ian glanced at her, "Was Lily Greenwood a friend of yours?"

She nodded, her voice soft. "We were childhood friends. I still remember the day they found her... the village hasn't been the same since."

The detective, ever observant, noticed the pain in her eyes. "I'm sorry for bringing up painful memories, but any insight you can provide could help in solving this puzzle."

They wandered through the unkempt gardens, past statues covered in moss and fountains long dry. "Lily loved this garden," Agatha reminisced. "We used to play here, imagining ourselves as queens of a fairy kingdom."

Arriving at the lake, Ian felt an inexplicable chill. The water was still, but the reflection of the looming mansion made it seem foreboding. Agatha pointed to a boathouse on the lake's edge, "She was found there, floating next to that boathouse."

Ian walked closer, inspecting the boathouse. Although most items inside had been covered with tarps and layers of dust, one item caught his eye: a locket, its chain tangled with some old fishing nets. Picking it up, he found a picture inside – a young, smiling Lily with a younger girl, presumably Agatha.

Agatha gasped as Ian showed her the locket. "That's the locket she wore every day! It was a gift from her mother. But... it went missing after her death. No one knew where it was."

The detective's mind raced. "If this was with her the day she died, why was it left here, tangled in these nets?"

As they pondered, Agatha recalled an old memory. "There was a letter, one that Lily wrote but never sent. I found it in her room after her death. It was addressed to Eleanor's father."

Ian's eyebrows shot up. "Do you remember what was in the letter?"

Agatha hesitated, struggling to remember. "It was years ago, but she mentioned something about meeting someone at the boathouse the evening she died. She seemed... worried."

The weight of the revelation hung in the air. "This isn't just a land dispute," Ian concluded. "This is about betrayal, hidden truths, and a young life cut short."

He carefully pocketed the locket, knowing it might be the key to unraveling the twisted tale that connected the Ellis family, the Lynches, and the tragic fate of Lily Greenwood.

Chapter 11

Shadows of Betrayal

The sun began its descent, casting the Greenwood estate in hues of orange and gold. The beauty of the moment was in stark contrast to the grim discoveries of the day. Detective McAllister and Agatha sat on a weathered stone bench, overlooking the lake where Lily met her untimely end.

"There's more to the story, isn't there?" Ian probed gently, seeing the far-off look in Agatha's eyes.

She took a deep breath, her fingers playing with the silver locket. "It wasn't just about the estate. It's about the relationships that intertwined our families. Lily, Eleanor, and I, we were inseparable as children. But as we grew older, alliances shifted, and promises were broken."

Ian waited, allowing her to collect her thoughts.

"Lily was smitten with a young man from the village, Peter," Agatha began. "He was charming, witty, and full of dreams. They were planning a future together. But there were whispers... rumors that Peter was also close to Eleanor. No one knew the depth of their relationship, but Lily was devastated."

Detective McAllister leaned forward. "Was Peter's relationship with Eleanor confirmed?"

Agatha nodded. "One evening, I saw them. They were by the edge of this very lake, holding each other close, lost in their world. The look in their eyes said it all. I never told Lily, fearing it would shatter her."

Ian's mind raced. The pieces of the puzzle were coming together, but there were still gaps. "Could Peter have been the person Lily was meeting at the boathouse?"

"It's possible," Agatha whispered, tears glistening in her eyes. "But what haunts me is that letter. She wanted to confide in someone, and she chose Eleanor's father. Why him?"

Ian pondered this. "If Eleanor's father was aware of the rendezvous, it could imply he had knowledge of the circumstances surrounding Lily's death. But it also suggests he was more than just a bystander in the affairs of the younger generation."

Agatha nodded in agreement. "There's a lot we never understood or saw. But one thing's for sure: the events of that fateful night have left their mark on all our families. The Lynches, the Greenwoods, the Ellises... none were left untouched."

As the evening drew closer, the shadows of the estate seemed to stretch out, as if trying to envelop the two in the secrets of the past. Ian stood up, determination in his eyes.

"We will uncover the truth, Agatha," he vowed. "For Lily, for the village, and for all the lives entangled in this tragedy."

The night had begun to settle in, but for Detective McAllister, the quest for answers was far from over.

Chapter 12

A Rendezvous at the Swan

Grasmere, though small, boasted a cozy little pub named 'The Swan.' Frequented by locals and tourists alike, it was a treasure trove of stories and gossip. And it was to this establishment that Detective McAllister decided to go next, hoping to glean more about the elusive Peter and his relationship with the two girls.

The rustic interior of 'The Swan' exuded warmth, with its polished wood tables, a roaring fireplace, and old photographs adorning the walls. Ian spotted a few elderly locals huddled in a corner, deep in conversation, their laughter echoing in the room.

He ordered a pint and took a seat at the bar, striking up a conversation with the bartender, Tom, a stout man with a bushy beard. "Evening, sir. Haven't seen you around. You new to Grasmere?"

"Just visiting," Ian replied. "Investigating an old matter, actually. You wouldn't happen to know anything about a Peter who was close to both Lily Greenwood and Eleanor?"

Tom's jovial expression changed momentarily, replaced with a pensive look. "Ah, Peter. Aye, he was quite the charmer back in the day. Broke many a heart, including Lily's, from what I've heard."

A woman sitting a few stools down, her grey hair pulled back in a neat bun, chimed in. "Peter was bad news. My sister knew him well. He was with Lily, but he also had eyes for Eleanor. Caused quite the stir, that one."

Ian leaned in, intrigued. "Do you know where he is now?"

She shook her head. "Left Grasmere not long after Lily's... incident. Some said he couldn't bear the guilt, while others believed he had something to hide."

Tom added, "There were rumors, you see. Whispers that he met Lily at the boathouse that night."

A chill ran down Ian's spine. The pieces were connecting, but the picture was far from complete. "Did Peter have any connection to the Lynches?"

The woman scoffed, "Who didn't, back then? The Lynches had their fingers in every pie. Peter worked for them for a time, handling some of their properties. It's why many believed they had a hand in what happened to Lily."

Ian took a moment to process this information. The web was more tangled than he had imagined. "Thank you," he said, leaving a tip for Tom. "You've given me a lot to think about."

As he left 'The Swan,' the weight of the past bore down on him. Grasmere's serene beauty hid a labyrinth of secrets and betrayals, and Detective McAllister was determined to navigate through it, no matter the cost.

$\mathcal{C}$hapter 13

Unearthing the Past

The following morning, Grasmere was bathed in soft sunlight, the gentle rays piercing through the gaps between the cottages and dappling the streets. It seemed like a different world in the daytime, the shadows of the previous night's revelations momentarily pushed away.

Ian found himself outside an old, quaint bookshop, its sign reading 'Baxter's Tales & Histories.' The store, with its promise of old town records and newspapers, was an investigative goldmine.

Inside, the smell of aged paper greeted him. Rows upon rows of books lined the shelves, and atop a worn-out counter sat a bespectacled old man, Mr. Baxter, the owner.

"Morning, sir," Ian greeted. "I'm hoping to look at old newspapers, specifically from around the time of Lily Greenwood's death."

Mr. Baxter squinted at him through thick glasses. "Researching the past, are you? That was a dark time for Grasmere."

Ian nodded. "It's crucial I uncover what happened."

Mr. Baxter led him to a back room filled with dusty archives. "Here we are. Grasmere's memories, both good and bad."

As Ian sifted through articles, an old photograph caught his eye. It depicted a group of young people, laughing and joyful. Among them were Lily, Eleanor, and a handsome young man Ian assumed was Peter.

"What can you tell me about this?" Ian asked, showing the photograph to Mr. Baxter.

The old man sighed, adjusting his glasses. "That was taken at the Grasmere summer fair. It was the last time we saw Lily genuinely happy. The young man there is Peter, as you might've guessed. Quite the trio they were. But soon after this, everything changed."

Ian's curiosity was piqued. "How so?"

"Well," Mr. Baxter hesitated, "it was evident to some of us that Peter was torn between the two ladies. Eleanor, with her family's influence, was a catch. But Lily... she had an innocence, a charm that was irresistible."

"Did Peter have ties to the Lynch family beyond his relationship with Eleanor?"

Mr. Baxter nodded slowly. "He did. He managed some of their estates. But there were rumors that he got involved in their darker dealings. Some even whispered he owed them money."

"And after Lily's death?"

"Peter was devastated," the shopkeeper said, his voice full of empathy. "Whether it was guilt or sorrow, no one truly knows. He left Grasmere soon after, trying to outrun the ghosts, I reckon."

Ian thanked Mr. Baxter, leaving the store with more questions than answers. As he wandered the streets, he couldn't shake off the feeling that he was close, so close, to unraveling the mystery. Grasmere's serene facade was slowly lifting, revealing a world of tangled relationships and long-buried secrets.

Chapter 14

Whispers in the Wind

The day had been long, but for Ian, sleep was elusive. His mind raced with the faces and stories of Grasmere's haunting past. The local inn, 'The Dove's Rest,' became his sanctuary for the night. Its ancient stone walls bore silent witness to many tales, and tonight, it would listen to one more.

At the inn's bustling tavern, Ian found himself seated next to a fire, nursing a drink. The flickering flames cast dancing shadows, reminiscent of the very shadows he was chasing.

A woman, around his age with raven-black hair, took the seat next to him. "Detective McAllister?" she asked, her voice soft yet firm.

Ian looked up, surprised. "Yes, and you are?"

"Evelyn," she introduced herself. "Evelyn Moore. I knew Lily. We were close, before... everything."

Ian leaned forward, sensing the importance of this meeting. "What can you tell me?"

She hesitated, taking a deep breath. "It's not just what happened to Lily that torments this town. It's the secrets, the alliances, the betrayals. Peter was at the heart of it, but he wasn't the puppet master."

Ian furrowed his brow. "Who was?"

Evelyn's gaze wavered. "The Lynches had influence, yes, but there was someone else. Someone from the shadows, pulling strings, orchestrating events."

Ian felt a chill. "Do you know who?"

Evelyn shook her head, her eyes glistening with tears. "I wish I did. All I know is, the night Lily died, and she had been planning to meet someone. Someone who had promised her answers, to expose the puppeteer. But she never got the chance."

"Was it Peter she was meeting?"

"No," Evelyn whispered, "I believe she was meeting someone from the Lynch family. Not Eleanor, but perhaps her father or uncle."

Ian pondered her words. The story was getting murkier. "Why are you telling me this now?"

"Because," Evelyn's voice wavered, "I can't bear the weight of this silence any longer. Grasmere needs to heal, and for that, the truth must come out. Just... be careful, Detective. Some secrets are guarded zealously."

With that, Evelyn left, leaving Ian with more questions. The fire in the hearth slowly died out, but the fire in Ian's determination blazed brighter than ever. He knew he was on the precipice of a breakthrough, but at what cost?

Grasmere's whispered secrets were beckoning, and he was ready to listen.

Chapter 15

The Lynch Legacy

With the dawn of a new day, Ian decided to head straight to the heart of the enigma: the Lynch estate. Nestled on the outskirts of Grasmere, the sprawling manor was emblematic of the family's vast influence and wealth.

A wrought-iron gate adorned with the Lynch family crest guarded the entrance. As Ian approached, an older gentleman with sharp, calculating eyes greeted him.

"Can I help you?" the man inquired, sizing up the detective.

"I'm Detective McAllister. I'd like to speak with a member of the Lynch family."

The man's expression barely changed. "I am Raymond Lynch, Eleanor's uncle. What business do you have with my family?"

Ian took a deep breath. "I'm investigating the circumstances surrounding Lily Greenwood's death. Recent revelations have hinted at your family's possible involvement."

Raymond's lips twitched into a faint smirk. "Ah, the past does have a way of catching up, doesn't it? Come, walk with me."

The two men strolled through the estate's manicured gardens. The beauty around them contrasted starkly with the gravity of their conversation.

"You must understand," Raymond began, "Our family has been at the helm of Grasmere's growth for generations. Such responsibility often requires... discretion."

Ian eyed him carefully. "Are you saying your family had something to hide regarding Lily's death?"

Raymond stopped, turning to face the detective. "Lily was a lovely girl, but she got entangled in a web much larger than herself. Peter was a pawn, as were many others."

Ian's patience wore thin. "I need direct answers, Mr. Lynch. Was your family involved?"

Raymond sighed, looking out over the lake in the distance. "My brother, Eleanor's father, did meet with Lily that night. She had discovered some... financial irregularities related to our estates. Peter, being in charge of certain transactions, was implicated. She believed we were defrauding locals out of their rightful property. But before she could expose anything, she died."

"And your brother?"

Raymond's eyes darkened. "He had every reason to silence Lily, but he swore to his dying day that he didn't harm her. He wanted to resolve matters quietly. He met her at the boathouse, but by the time he got there, she was already..."

Ian felt the pieces aligning. "Was Peter aware of this?"

Raymond hesitated. "He knew of the irregularities, but not of my brother's intended meeting with Lily. In his grief, he left Grasmere, unaware of the extent of the chaos he left behind."

Ian processed the information. "So, if your brother didn't harm Lily, who did?"

Raymond looked at Ian, his gaze intense. "That's the question that's haunted this family for years. We've lived under the shadow of suspicion, but the true culprit remains hidden."

The weight of Raymond's revelation settled heavily on Ian's shoulders. The path to truth was proving to be more intricate than he'd imagined, but he was undeterred. The detective was closer than ever to solving Grasmere's most haunting mystery.

Chapter 16

Ripples in Still Water

The Lynch estate, with its looming grandeur, felt suffocating after Raymond's revelations. Ian needed fresh air, a space to think. Grasmere Lake, with its reflective calm, seemed the perfect spot.

The lake, surrounded by gentle slopes and dappled sunlight, always had a way of calming Ian's thoughts. He settled on a secluded bench, pulling out his notes, piecing together the narrative. Raymond's words echoed in his mind. If Eleanor's father was not the culprit, then who was?

Lost in thought, he barely noticed a figure approaching him. It was Eleanor, her auburn hair reflecting the sun's hues.

"Ian," she began, her voice carrying a hint of nervousness. "I heard you visited our estate."

He nodded, looking up. "Your uncle shared some crucial information. But I feel there's more to the story. Something he's not telling me."

Eleanor hesitated before sitting next to him. "I was a child when it all happened, but the shadow of that night has always hung over our family. It's time I told you everything I know."

Ian turned to face her fully. "I'm listening."

She took a deep breath. "On the night Lily died, after she met my father, he returned home distraught, saying Lily had already been dead when he reached. I overheard him confide in my mother. He mentioned a letter, a note that Lily had on her. But when her belongings were returned, there was no letter."

Ian's interest piqued. "What did this letter contain?"

Eleanor shook her head. "I don't know. My father never spoke of it again. But I've always believed that if we find that letter, we'd discover the truth."

A realization dawned on Ian. "Someone got to Lily before your father did. Someone who didn't want that letter found."

Eleanor nodded, tears forming in her eyes. "I loved Lily like a sister. I never believed the rumors about my family, but now... it's hard not to doubt."

Ian placed a comforting hand on her shoulder. "We will uncover the truth, Eleanor. For Lily."

The two sat in silence for a moment, the tranquil ripples of the lake echoing the turmoil in their hearts.

Finally, Eleanor spoke, her voice barely a whisper. "I think my mother knows more. She's never spoken of it, but there have been nights I've heard her crying, whispering Lily's name. Maybe... maybe she can help you."

Ian felt another piece of the puzzle click into place. "Then I need to speak with her."

Eleanor nodded. "I'll arrange it. But please, be gentle with her. This mystery has already taken too much from us."

The still waters of Grasmere Lake hid many secrets. But with each passing day, Ian was determined to bring them to the surface. The ripples of the past would not remain still for much longer.

Chapter 17

Secrets of the Silent Matron

The Lynch manor looked even more imposing in the evening light. As Ian approached, he noticed the lights of the grand ballroom illuminating the grounds, painting shadows on the statues lining the path. The Lynch family was known for their lavish gatherings, but tonight the house seemed enveloped in an uneasy quiet.

Inside, Eleanor led Ian to a dimly lit study. On the far side, sitting in a high-back chair, was a distinguished older woman with silver streaks in her hair. Her gaze was sharp, but her eyes betrayed a deep sadness. This was Clarissa Lynch, Eleanor's mother.

"Mother," Eleanor began, her voice quivering slightly, "Detective McAllister is here to discuss the night Lily died."

Clarissa's gaze never wavered. "I was wondering when this day would come."

Ian cleared his throat. "Mrs. Lynch, any information you can provide will be invaluable."

She took a moment, then beckoned him to sit. "I loved Lily, you know. She was like a daughter I never had. What happened to her was a tragedy that has haunted our family."

Ian leaned forward, sensing the significance of the conversation. "Eleanor mentioned a letter. One that was never found among Lily's belongings."

A tear slid down Clarissa's cheek. "That letter... it was meant to be a secret. Lily had discovered discrepancies in our family accounts, transactions she couldn't reconcile. She wrote to a close confidante about her suspicions, fearing for her life."

"Who was this confidante?" Ian pressed.

Clarissa hesitated. "It was me."

Ian was taken aback. "You?"

She nodded. "Lily didn't trust many, but she trusted me. She gave me the letter for safekeeping a day before she died. I never disclosed it to protect my family's name and to shield my daughter from the painful truth."

Ian felt a mix of frustration and sympathy. "What was in the letter?"

Clarissa took a deep breath. "It named several individuals in Grasmere, influential ones, who were involved in shady land deals. Lily had inadvertently discovered their schemes. Peter's name was mentioned, but as a pawn. There were bigger players at work. She believed her life was in danger."

Ian processed this. "The letter could be the key to solving the case. Do you still have it?"

Clarissa nodded slowly. "I've kept it hidden all these years, hoping to protect the ones I love."

Eleanor, hearing this, looked distraught. "Mother, why didn't you tell me?"

Clarissa reached out, gripping her daughter's hand. "I wanted to keep you safe, away from the darkness that surrounded that night."

Ian interjected, "We need that letter, Mrs. Lynch. It's vital evidence."

She paused, then finally whispered, "I will retrieve it for you."

As Clarissa left the room, Ian and Eleanor exchanged glances, both sensing the weight of the impending revelation. The secrets that Grasmere held were slowly unraveling, layer by layer, and Ian knew he was drawing closer to the heart of the mystery.

Chapter 18

Whispers of the Past

The grandfather clock in the corner of the study ticked away the minutes, its monotonous rhythm amplifying the tension in the room. Eleanor looked conflicted, wringing her hands in apprehension, while Ian impatiently tapped his fingers on the armrest.

When Clarissa returned, she held a worn, sealed envelope. Handing it over, she whispered, "This has been a heavy burden. I hope it brings Lily the justice she deserves."

Ian carefully opened the letter, its fragile pages bearing the weight of years and secrets. Eleanor leaned in, both of them reading the beautifully scripted words:

"Dearest Clarissa,

If you are reading this, it means my fears were not unfounded. I've discovered something alarming. Peter, unknowingly, has been used as a scapegoat in a scheme by some influential members of Grasmere. Names like Lord Harrington, Councilman Wyatt, and even... I fear mentioning this... Richard Turner, the local banker.

I intend to confront them, and demand answers. But I need you to know, should anything happen to me, these names are involved. Protect Peter. He's innocent in all this.

Forever grateful for your friendship,

Lily."

Eleanor gasped, covering her mouth. "Richard Turner? He's one of Grasmere's most respected figures!"

Ian's expression was grim. "A respected figure with a motive. If Lily had gone public, his reputation would have been destroyed."

Clarissa spoke up, her voice trembling, "After Lily's death, I did notice Richard acting peculiarly. He'd visit our estate frequently, inquiring about any letters or documents Lily might have left behind."

Eleanor looked horrified. "You think he's behind this? That he's the one who silenced Lily?"

Ian rubbed his chin thoughtfully. "It's a possibility. But we need more evidence. Mrs. Lynch, did Richard know about this letter's existence?"

Clarissa hesitated, then admitted, "He might have overheard Lily mentioning it to me once, but I'm not certain."

Ian stood up, determination in his eyes. "We need to investigate Richard Turner further, understand his connections, and see if there's any evidence linking him directly to that fateful night."

Eleanor nodded, her resolve strengthening. "I'm with you, Ian. Lily deserves justice, and if Richard Turner is behind this, he won't get away with it."

Clarissa, watching them, felt a mix of fear and hope. The ghosts of the past were awakening, and she prayed they'd finally find peace.

As Ian and Eleanor left the Lynch manor, the night shrouded Grasmere in its embrace. But there was a promise of dawn, a hint of truth breaking through the darkness. The next steps were crucial, and Ian knew the path would be fraught with danger.

Chapter 19

The Banker's Betrayal

The next day, Ian and Eleanor found themselves in the heart of Grasmere's financial district. Towering over the other establishments was the edifice of Turner Bank, its neo-gothic architecture a testament to its age and prominence.

They entered, the marble floor echoing their footsteps, drawing the attention of the tellers and patrons. A large portrait of Richard Turner, exuding confidence and charm, hung prominently on one wall. Under different circumstances, no one would suspect the charismatic banker to harbor such dark secrets.

"I'll handle this," Ian whispered to Eleanor as he approached the reception desk. "Miss, I'd like to speak to Mr. Turner."

The receptionist looked Ian up and down, skepticism evident in her eyes. "Do you have an appointment?"

Ian flashed his badge. "Detective McAllister. It's urgent."

The receptionist hesitated for a moment, then picked up her phone. After a brief conversation, she looked up, "Mr. Turner will see you now. His office is on the top floor."

Ascending the grand staircase, the duo felt the weight of the opulence around them. But Eleanor's thoughts were consumed by the possibility of Richard's involvement. A childhood friend, someone she'd looked up to.

Richard's office door was ajar. As they approached, they overheard a heated conversation.

"I told you to handle it! Now they're sniffing around here!" Richard's voice was laced with anger.

A second, unfamiliar voice responded, "We took care of the girl, didn't we? Just give it time, Richard. Things will cool down."

Richard retorted, "Every minute that detective is in Grasmere, our entire operation is at risk!"

Ian decided it was time to make an entrance. He knocked sharply, pushing the door open. Richard's face paled upon seeing them, while his companion, a tall, burly man with a scar running down his cheek, looked equally surprised.

"Detective McAllister," Richard began, trying to regain his composure. "To what do I owe the pleasure?"

Ian wasted no time. "We have evidence pointing to some unsavory dealings you might be involved in. Care to explain?"

Richard laughed, feigning innocence. "You're barking up the wrong tree, detective."

Eleanor stepped forward, anger evident in her voice. "We have a letter, Richard. Lily's letter."

The color drained from Richard's face. His companion, sensing the change in the room, began inching towards the exit.

Ian, however, was one step ahead. Drawing his gun, he ordered, "Stay right there. Both of you."

The burly man froze, hands raised.

"Richard," Eleanor implored, "tell us the truth. For old times' sake."

Richard looked defeated, his bravado replaced by guilt. "I didn't want her dead. But she knew too much."

Ian's gaze hardened. "So you had her killed."

Richard's voice trembled. "Not directly. I told some associates about the situation. They promised to 'handle it.' I never imagined..."

The weight of the revelation hung in the air. Eleanor's sense of betrayal was palpable. Grasmere's prominent banker was not just involved in shady deals but was now implicated in Lily's death.

As the cuffs clicked around Richard's wrists, Ian whispered to Eleanor, "Justice is close, but we need to tread carefully. There's still more to this than meets the eye."

$\mathcal{C}$hapter 20

Web of Deceit

The Grasmere police station was abuzz with activity. Officers moved back and forth, papers rustled, and phones rang incessantly. At the center of this hive, in an interrogation room, sat Richard Turner. The dim light from the single overhead bulb cast shadows across his once-confident face, now marred with worry.

Outside the room, Ian briefed the chief. "We have Turner, but there's more to this. His associate – the one we found in his office – goes by the name of Victor Kline. Records show he's got ties to organized crime up north."

The chief, a stout, grizzled man named Donald Wallace, rubbed his temples. "This is bigger than we imagined. If Kline's involved, we're dealing with dangerous people."

Ian nodded, "We need to unravel this quickly, Chief. Before they realize Turner's in custody and come after him... or us."

Wallace looked at Ian with genuine concern. "Be careful, Ian. These aren't small-time crooks."

Eleanor, having overheard the conversation, approached. "What can I do to help?"

Ian looked at her, admiration evident in his eyes. "We need to delve deeper into Turner's financial records, see who else might be involved."

Within the hour, Eleanor had arranged a thorough search of Turner Bank's records. As the trio pored over them in an improvised operation room, patterns began to emerge.

"These transactions," Eleanor pointed out, "they're transfers to a shell company, but they're massive sums. And look, the dates coincide with the days leading up to Lily's death."

Ian leaned in, examining the details. "Lakeside Properties Ltd. Never heard of them. But this... this is our lead."

Just then, an officer rushed in, a panicked look on his face. "Detective McAllister, there's been an incident."

Ian and Eleanor exchanged worried glances. "What happened?"

The officer gulped. "Victor Kline. He's been found dead in his cell."

A chill ran down Ian's spine. "They're cleaning up loose ends."

Wallace looked grim. "We need to move fast. Every minute counts now."

Eleanor, her resolve unwavering, said, "Let's go back to the letter. If we follow the money, we can find the head of this snake."

Hours turned into a whirlwind of cross-referencing, phone calls, and revelations. The night aged, and as dawn broke, Eleanor discovered the final piece of the puzzle.

"Look at this," she said, her voice filled with a mixture of triumph and dread. "The major shareholder of Lakeside Properties Ltd. is none other than... Councilman Wyatt."

Ian looked up, realization dawning. "The same Wyatt from Lily's letter. This goes all the way to the top."

Wallace, lighting a cigar, remarked, "We've got a lot of work ahead, but at least now we know our enemy."

As the first light of day filtered through the blinds, Ian felt a renewed sense of purpose. Grasmere's darkest secrets were beginning to see the light, and justice, though delayed, was on the horizon.

Epilogue

Dawn Over Grasmere

Three months had passed since the revelations at Turner Bank. The small town of Grasmere was forever changed. The headlines shook the very core of the community, revealing the corrupt ties that bound the town's elite.

Councilman Wyatt was arrested, his political career in shambles. With overwhelming evidence against him, the trial was swift. His connections, once a protective shield, were now his downfall. He was sentenced to life imprisonment, with no chance of parole.

Richard Turner, although not directly responsible for Lily's death, couldn't escape his own sins. The court showed no leniency for his involvement with organized crime. He was sentenced to twenty years in prison.

Eleanor took over the Lakeside Bistro, turning it into a thriving hub of community and remembrance. She established "Lily's Corner", a small section of the restaurant dedicated to her friend, filled with pictures, poems, and memories of happier times.

Ian McAllister received accolades for his dedication to the case. However, the shadows of Grasmere still weighed on him. He transferred to a quieter district, seeking peace and a fresh start.

Clarissa Lynch, with the truth unveiled, finally found solace. The weight of the secret letter had been lifted. She turned her estate into a sanctuary for troubled youth, ensuring that Lily's legacy would be one of hope and redemption.

Grasmere, though scarred, began to heal. The community came together like never before, building a brighter future on the foundations of the past.

On the anniversary of Lily's death, a memorial was erected by the lake, a symbol of resilience and remembrance. Every year, residents gather, candles in hand, to honor the girl whose tragic end brought to light the darkness lurking in the shadows.

As the sun set on another day in Grasmere, the serene waters of the lake reflected the town's restored peace. The storm had passed, and a new dawn awaited.

Printed in Great Britain
by Amazon

44259075R00036